Andy was born and raised in the east end of London. He went to Parmiter's Grammar School and started working at age 15. Andy started his own company and eventually employed over a 100 people. Later, he sold out to a South African company in 2001 and retired.

CHARLIE
ANT

ANDY HUXTABLE

THE CAKE

AUSTIN MACAULEY PUBLISHERS™
LONDON · CAMBRIDGE · NEW YORK · SHARJAH

ISBN 9781528916561 (Paperback)
ISBN 9781528916578 (Hardback)
ISBN 9781528961608 (ePub e-book)

www.austinmacauley.com

First Published (2020)
Austin Macauley Publishers Ltd
25 Canada Square
Canary Wharf
London
E14 5LQ

For Liam, Shiloh and Lois, without whom this book would never have been written.

Number 14 Sunny Avenue was a house pretty much like every other house in the street. It had a small front garden and a small back garden with a stone patio just outside the kitchen door.

At the bottom of the garden was a small brook which rippled across stones and tree roots and meandered its way to the next village. Beyond the brook was a large field with some cows and sometimes sheep were kept there to graze for a short time before being moved on to another field somewhere else.

All in all, it was a fairly ordinary house but with one exception! Underneath the stone patio outside the kitchen door was an ant colony...this was where Charlie Ant lived.

Charlie had always lived there, at least he thought he had. He didn't ever remember 'moving' there, in fact, he didn't even remember being born there! It had always been the same for Charlie, this was his home and he loved it.

Charlie Ant was most unlike any other ant. He did have six legs, but he would always keep his two middle legs in his pockets as he never used them. He never walked on six legs, he chose to only walk on two of them! He found this so much easier and, although not quite as fast as walking on six legs, he preferred being taller and slower than all the other ants who just busied themselves running up and down the tunnels carrying leaves. Sam, who was Charlie's best friend, walked the same way as Charlie so it made them both the 'odd ants out' in the colony. None of the other ants ever took any notice anyway as they were always far too busy to stop, and talk, let alone ask questions.

Charlie lived just off the main tunnel in room number 7 and Sam lived right next door to him in number 8. Directly opposite their rooms was room number 1, the Queen Ant's room. Charlie and Sam just happened to be the Queen's favorites.

The reason for them being her favorites was probably because they appeared much taller as they walked on two legs rather than six! This made them stand out from all the others and funnily enough made them seem much cleverer too!

They also lived the closest to the Queen, so they were very useful to her when she wanted something other than feeding or having all her eggs looked after.

Charlie and Sam had never ever carried leaves and had never ever looked after any eggs, there were far too many other ants to do all that sort of stuff and even so, Charlie much preferred exploring and going on his little adventures!

This particular morning, Charlie had just woken up and was having a lovely stretchy yawn while sitting on the edge of his bed when suddenly, the door flew open and Sam came crashing through it so quickly that he tripped over the mat, did a double somersault and landed with a thud on the floor!

9

'Sam, can you at least knock before coming in, you made me jump then,' said Charlie.

'Sorry Charlie,' muttered Sam rubbing his head. 'But we've been summoned in to see the Queen straight away, so I had to get you quickly.'

'Really?' said Charlie, 'I wonder what she wants?'

'I have no idea,' replied Sam, 'but hurry up Charlie, let's go.'

Charlie jumped up from his bed and followed Sam out of the door and across the tunnel to room number 1. Sam gently knocked on the door and heard a voice from inside which said, quite simply, 'Come'.

Charlie opened the door gently and they both stepped inside as quietly as they could.

'Charlie,' the Queen began, 'I need your help today with just a little something.'

'Of course, Your Majesty,' answered Charlie respectfully. 'What can we help you with?'

'It is a little embarrassing Charlie,' replied the Queen, 'and I would rather you kept this to yourselves and NOT mention it to anyone else!'

'That goes without saying, Your Majesty,' replied Charlie, 'we hardly ever talk to the other ants anyway, unless we need their help with something.'

'You shall do this on your own,' ordered the Queen, 'with no mention to anyone, and that includes the Wizard Ant! Now, be seated and listen up.'

11

Charlie and Sam sat down immediately and listened. It wasn't a good thing to make the Queen angry at any time, as she could get really nasty and make them walk on six legs!

The Queen began to speak, 'Okay, I've been eating leaves for years and although they are quite yummy, one has had enough of leaves and one has been dreaming lately of cake!' As she spoke, she seemed to drift away dreamily and her eyes were staring into empty space. Charlie thought he saw a little dribble around her mouth but said nothing. 'I want you to get me some cake today, now...yes, right now. Chocolate cake, yes...chocolate cake, not fruit cake, not Victoria sponge cake...ONLY chocolate cake! Do you understand? Chocolate CAKE,' she shouted. 'NOW GO!'

Sam and Charlie jumped to their feet and zoomed out of the door as quickly as they could. Their mission had begun!

'Charlie, where on earth are we going to find chocolate cake?
'asked Sam.

'I think I have an idea,' replied Charlie. 'Follow me Sam.'

Now, unless you are an ant yourself, you probably won't realise that ant tunnels are extremely busy places! There are ants going up and down the tunnels most of the day and night, carrying leaves on the way in and empty handed on the way out. Charlie and Sam had to wait for a gap in the ants before they could start their journey!

They both turned right outside the Queen's room, waited for a gap and jumped in. They walked up the long tunnel which led outside to the garden. As they walked, they saw in the distance, a bright speck of daylight that was the entrance to the ant colony. It wasn't a long walk, they had done this many times before and were always excited when they were going out into the big wide world where the big people were.

14

There were rules about being where big people were but the most important rule was 'not to get stepped on'. They had seen lots of the other ants get stepped on before and those ants had ended up quite flat and very still and didn't carry leaves anymore. This didn't seem to be very good to Sam and Charlie so they stayed well away from big people. They also stayed well away from cats and dogs as they had also seen other ants being 'sniffed up' their noses and never come back again!

As they came out of the tunnel entrance, the bright sun made them shield their eyes. Ants are not really used to bright sunlight as they spend most of the day in their dark tunnels. It didn't take long for Charlie and Sam to get used to the sun and soon they were making their way across the stone patio towards the kitchen door. 'What's the plan, Charlie?' asked Sam

'Look Sam, big people eat cake, don't they? Big people get cake from shops and big people live in houses, don't they? So I think if we go into some houses we will find cake!' Sam thought Charlie was just so amazing, he was really clever and seemed to have all the answers.

'That's a great plan, Charlie,' said Sam. 'So what house do we go into?'

'All of them,' replied Charlie, 'yes, all of them...until we find a chocolate cake.'

It is actually very easy for an ant to get into a house as they are so small. There are always little cracks and holes to get in by and sometimes the big people leave the doors open for their pets to get in and out of. So, getting in was easy but the problem was going to be getting out carrying a cake, a chocolate cake...

Ants may be small but they are all extremely strong, so carrying a cake wasn't too difficult but carrying a cake 'without being seen' was!

Charlie had decided that the first thing to do was to find the right cake and then once the cake was found, he would figure out a plan to remove it from the house and get it to the queen in one piece!

'Okay Sam, follow me and keep close,' said Charlie. Sam followed, he always did what Charlie said.

The two of them headed straight to the kitchen door which, luckily enough, was already open. They went in and looked around slowly. There was a small fluffy white dog asleep in a basket between two cupboards but no big people around.

Ants are quiet, so they probably wouldn't wake the dog by walking or talking, it would only be the sound of cupboard doors opening and shutting that would make any noise, so they had to do that carefully and quietly.

They decided not to open the doors but just to creep in each one through the little gaps until they found the cake that the Queen wanted. This was quicker and easier and within five minutes, they had been in and out of every cupboard in the kitchen without finding what they were looking for. Sam however had found a nice bowl of sugar which he decided to lay in for a while, he loved sugar and he played with the tiny little white grains for quite a while before Charlie found him. He had also eaten quite a lot of it and was feeling a little bit sick and wasn't happy about Charlie telling him to get out of the bowl and get on with the job!

18

As they started to walk out of the kitchen, Sam spat a little grain of sugar out of his mouth which hit the fluffy white dog right on its nose. The dog slowly opened one of its eyes and instantly closed it again.

'Sam, please don't do that,' said Charlie, 'you could get us both sniffed up its nose!'

'Sorry,' replied Sam miserably, he really was feeling sick from all that sugar and just wanted to get home to lay down on his bed for a while.

'Right,' said Charlie cheerfully, 'next house is under the fence, let's try that one.'

Sam followed without speaking, his tummy was aching, and he needed the toilet fast. They walked under the fence and Sam disappeared under a flower pot.

20

'Sam, what are you doing?' yelled Charlie, 'get back here now!'

'Can't,' called Sam from under the pot, 'you'll have to wait a little while for me.'

'What are you playing at, Sam?' said Charlie, 'We're on a mission for the Queen so stop being stupid.'

Sam said nothing...

'Sam,' called Charlie again, 'what are you doing?'

'Shush,' said Sam, 'I'm a bit busy at the moment.'

'What do you mean busy? Look Sam, there's no time to play silly games, this is important, now get out from under that flower pot right now!'

'Shush,' said Sam again, 'I'll be there in just a moment, aaahhhh that's better. Okay, I'm coming now.'

Sam popped out his head from under the flower pot and stared at Charlie, embarrassed.

'Sorry about that Charlie but I had to go, and quickly.'

'Go where?' asked Charlie.

'Toilet,' said Sam very quietly.

'WHAT?' shouted Charlie.

'Shush,' said Sam, 'I had to go to the toilet urgently.'

'Oh,' said Charlie, 'well, how many times have you been told not to eat sugar? You know what it does to your teeth, don't you? You know the najjers come at night and dig holes in your teeth, don't you? And you also know that it gives you an upset tummy, don't you? So, stop eating sugar Sam, otherwise we will never get the cake for the Queen.'

'Okay,' replied Sam totally embarrassed at being told off by his best friend.

They went into four more houses before they found exactly what they were looking for! There it was, freshly baked and sitting on the top of the kitchen table.

They stared at the chocolate topping which was running down the sides of the cake in smooth droplets covering the delicious chocolate sponge center.

Sam and Charlie started dribbling as they sniffed the chocolatey smell of this gorgeous cake which sat before them.

'Right,' said Charlie. 'Sam, go and have a look around to see if there are big people in the house, I'll figure out how we're going to get the cake out of the house'.

Sam went off and returned a few minutes later.

'There are two "small" big people sitting watching a television in the living room which I think they call "children", also, I think it is a "big people mummy" who is feeding a very small "baby big people" a bottle of white stuff? They all seem very busy, so I don't think they will see us for a while.'

'Great, Sam, thanks. I've got an idea, but we have to be really quiet. There are two brooms over there, come with me to fetch them.'

They got the brooms easily and put them against the table with the cake on to make a sort of "slide".

'Okay Sam, that's excellent. Now, you and I will push the cake to the edge of the table, we'll jump on the broom sticks and pull the cake towards us and then onto the broomsticks, then we'll slowly slide it down. It won't be heavy, but we must be careful not to go too fast, otherwise, it will slip and fall.'

'Okay Charlie, I understand, let's do it.'

They pushed the cake to the edge of the table and let it overhang a little, they moved the brooms into position just under the cake to make the slide and jumped onto the brooms. Pulling the cake onto the brooms was a little tricky and Charlie almost slipped and fell when a drop of chocolate fell onto his head, but they managed okay. Slowly but surely, they gradually let the cake slide down the broom sticks to the floor. Charlie managed to find two chopsticks which they carefully placed beneath the cake, they then pushed the cake across the kitchen floor towards the backdoor that led into the garden.

They were about four gardens away from where they started but managed to get the cake through the bushes and over the little fences without spoiling it too much.

More than once, they were attacked by wasps and flies who wanted their share of the cake but by the time they arrived at the entrance to the ant colony, the cake was looking quite good.

They soon realised that ant holes are not quite big enough to get a chocolate cake through and this was most definitely going to be a problem for them!

'It will never fit down there,' said Sam.

'I know,' replied Charlie. 'Well, if we can't get the cake to the Queen, we'll have to get the Queen to the cake! Wait here Sam and guard the cake with your life!'

Charlie rushed into the long dark tunnel until he reached room number 1. He knocked softly and heard a voice from inside which just said, 'Come'.

Charlie opened the door and saw the Queen on her throne staring into space.

'Your Majesty, I am pleased to tell you that Sam and I have found you a delicious chocolate cake. The problem is Your Majesty; we can't get it down the tunnel as it's way too big! May I suggest that you kindly make your way to the tunnel entrance where we have left it?'

The Queen did not answer straight away, she carried on staring into space as if she had not even heard what Charlie had said!

'Your Majesty?' began Charlie again.

'Shush Charlie, I'm thinking,' she commanded.

Charlie shushed, and waited patiently, he was hoping that the cake was safe with Sam and that Sam had not decided to make an early start on the cake by eating it himself.

'Charlie,' the Queen began to speak very slowly. 'Charlie, I have never ever been outside of this room. I eat, I lay eggs and I sit and I sleep here, it is all I have ever known! I need that cake Charlie but I cannot go out to get it, it MUST be brought to me!'

Charlie stood and thought how he could get the cake through the tunnels to the Queen's room. It was going to be impossible to get it into the tunnel in one piece, that was for sure. The only way was to get the worker ants to grab it piece by piece and carry it to the Queen as they did with the leaves.

He told the Queen exactly what he was thinking and although she desperately wanted to see the cake in one big piece, she also realised that even Charlie couldn't do the impossible. She had no choice but to agree to what he suggested.

'Okay Charlie, I understand, it's a shame that you couldn't find a cake which would fit into the tunnel but you have done your best. Get the worker ants to help and carry it piece by piece to my room. I will tell you when I have eaten enough and then you can stop.'

Charlie rushed back out of the tunnel to give Sam the message. When he arrived at the entrance, he saw Sam's head buried deep inside the chocolate topping of the cake! He couldn't believe his eyes; Sam had started to eat the Queen's cake!

'SAM!' Charlie screamed. 'Get your head OUT of that cake right now!!!'

With a huge PLOP, Sam's head emerged from the gooey mess he had made with his head. His whole face, including his scrawny little ant neck, was covered with chocolate, he looked a complete mess and so did the cake. He stared at Charlie for a moment, looked back at the cake and then burst into tears.

'What on earth do you think you are doing?' screamed Charlie. 'You are eating the Queen's cake!'

Sam was sobbing his little heart out, unable to speak. Charlie sat down on the floor not knowing what to do.

At that very moment, the Queen's head popped out of the ant tunnel...

Charlie and Sam stared at each other and then at the Queen as she slowly made her way towards the cake. Her eyes were bulging at the sight of that delicious cake standing in front of her. Her nose was full of the smell of chocolate. She hadn't noticed that Sam was sitting on top of the cake covered in chocolate, she hadn't noticed Charlie sitting down beside the cake looking very scared.

With one giant leap, she jumped into the middle of the cake and immediately started to gobble it up!

Charlie stared at her, Sam stopped sobbing and stared at her as she munched her way through that lovely cake, not even noticing that Sam and Charlie were there. When she had eaten most of the cake, she lay on her back and let out an enormous BURP.

Charlie knew that Sam was out of trouble as the Queen hadn't even noticed him. She was so hungry for that cake that she didn't see that Sam had already been eating it, so he wouldn't be in trouble either.

The only problem now was to get the Queen back into the tunnel and into her room.

She had eaten so much that she was now twice the size that she was! Unfortunately, as much as they tugged and pulled, they could not get her back inside the tunnel and the poor Queen had to wait for a week outside in the wind and rain before she was small enough to return to her room...

CPSIA information can be obtained
at www.ICGtesting.com
Printed in the USA
LVHW071459070322
712831LV00008B/267